馬
Horse

Sheep

猴
Monkey

蛇
Snake

雞
Rooster

龍
Dragon

For nearly 5,000 years, the Chinese culture
has organized time in cycles of twelve years.
This Eastern calendar is based upon the movement
of the moon (as compared to the Western calendar
which follows the sun's path). The zodiac circle symbolizes
how animals, which have unique qualities, represent each
year. Therefore, if you are born in a particular year,
then you share the personality of that animal.
Now people worldwide celebrate this fifteen-day
festival in the early spring and enjoy the
start of another Chinese New Year.

狗
Dog

兔
Rabbit

豬
Pig

虎
Tiger

牛
Ox

鼠
Rat

To the growing branches of my family tree, such as my sister-in-law Christine Wong and cousins Richard Wing, Valerie Lim, and Stephanie Chu.
—O.C.

This book is dedicated to Coconuts, who is my inspiration for Sydney!
—A.C.

immedium

Immedium, Inc.
P.O. Box 31846
San Francisco, CA 94131
www.immedium.com

First hardcover edition published 2015.

Edited by Don Menn
Book design by Erica Loh Jones
Calligraphy by Lucy Chu

Printed in Malaysia
10 9 8 7 6 5 4 3 2 1

Library of Congress Cataloging-in-Publication Data

Chin, Oliver Clyde, 1969- author.
 The year of the sheep : tales from the Chinese zodiac / by Oliver Chin ; illustrated by Alina Chau. -- First hardcover edition.
    pages cm
 Summary: "The lamb Sydney befriends the shepherd girl Zhi, as well as other animals of the Chinese lunar calendar, and demonstrates the qualities of a kind heart. Lists the birth years and characteristics of individuals born in the Chinese Year of the Sheep"-- Provided by publisher.
 ISBN 978-1-59702-104-3 (hardback) -- ISBN 1-59702-104-0 (hardcover)
 [1. Sheep--Fiction. 2. Astrology, Chinese--Fiction.] I. Chau, Alina, illustrator. II. Title.
 PZ7.C44235Yet 2015
 [E]--dc23
                                        2014008743

ISBN 978-1359702-104-3

The Year of the Sheep

Tales from the Chinese Zodiac

Written by Oliver Chin

Illustrated by Alina Chau

The sheep family celebrated the new year and brought a baby into their fold. Overjoyed, the ram and ewe named her Sydney.

Hungry for her first meal, the little lamb bleated, **"*Baaa Baaa!*"**

Nuzzling her soft parents, Sydney cuddled up for a comfy nap.
Members of their flock and other dear friends visited them.
Next arrived Zhi, the shepherds' daughter, and her dog Dao.

Zhi greeted Sydney cheerfully, "Hello, there!" The gals took a liking to each other right away.

Mama said, "The shepherds look after us and we take care of them."

"How so?" replied Sydney.

Papa explained, "Our coats keep us warm in winter and cool in summer. Every year we get haircuts and they make clothes from our wool."

Mama added, "We also provide them milk for drinking and making into cheese."

The next day Zhi led the flock out beyond the fence.
"Where are we going?" asked Sydney.

"We're heading to lunch," answered Zhi.

"My job is to make sure that
you're always well-fed!"

The sheep bunched together, since there was safety in numbers.
Papa advised, "Stay close and keep your eyes open and ears up."

They walked across the meadow
in a looping trail, like the
winding river nearby.

Zhi and Dao guided them toward spots of lush grass.
Spring had coaxed tender blades from the ground.
Sydney and her companions ate to their
heart's delight, then Zhi led them home.

The lambs liked to play the games "follow the leader" and "king of the hill."

Climbing on the grownups' backs, Sydney became a good hiker. But she thought, **"I want to explore off the beaten path."**

The following day the group took their regular walk. But Sydney smelled a sweet scent and strayed over the hill.

A good shepherd, Zhi called out, "Sydney, where are you?" But she didn't hear a peep.

Lured by the fresh fruit,
Sydney climbed an apple tree.
But she went too far out
on a limb and got stuck.
"Baaa Baaa!" she squealed.

Luckily Zhi heard her and came to the rescue.

Back at home Sydney admired the colorful flowers in the shepherds' garden.
She wondered, **"Do they taste as good as they look?"**

One day she noted that the gate was open.
So she snuck in for a closer peek.

Sydney began to nibble. Quickly she sampled the entire rainbow of flavors.

But just then Dao detected her and barked, "Hey, you don't belong in there!"

Shooed away, she scampered to rejoin the herd.

Later Sydney noticed the lovely lawn atop the shepherds' house.

With no one in sight, Sydney scrambled
onto the sod roof to graze. There
stood an odd column of bricks.
"What is this for?"
she thought.

Sydney peered down the chimney. Whoops! She slipped and fell through!

"Baaa Baaa!" she bawled.

Zhi plucked her from the dusty fireplace. Papa frowned, "Darling, can you stop getting into trouble?"

But soon dark clouds gathered overhead. The wind whipped through the forest and thunder shook the ground.

Zhi shouted, "Get to the barn!" There they stayed inside, for days on end, as the weather howled.

When the sky finally cleared, the land was quite a mess.

Worried they explored around. Oh no! They found their favorite patch of pasture had withered.

Sydney grumbled,
"These shoots are too hard to stomach."

Suddenly a tiger appeared. "Everyone run!" cried Zhi.

All the sheep fled... except Sydney. Where was she? The girl told Dao to herd the flock home, while she stayed behind to search for the little lost lamb.

Meanwhile, Sydney was around the bend talking with a rat. She followed him down to the river and discovered that the water was gone.

Surprised, she asked,
"What happened here?"
But no one knew.

Curious they tracked the trickle upstream. Eventually, they saw that a bundle of boulders and branches had blocked the river. Sydney reckoned, **"Hmm... that storm must have caused this logjam."**

Zhi finally spotted and scolded her, "What are you doing here?"

Sydney told Zhi what she had uncovered.

But night was approaching, so they hastily said goodbye to their new pals and sped home.

Sydney's parents were glad to see her but were very upset, too.
Mama moaned, "We were worried sick about you!"

Papa warned,
"Honey, don't wander off
by yourself anymore!"
Their daughter was
sheepish indeed.

However, the girls kept thinking about the river. The plants, animals, and people depended on water. But if the river ran dry, then everybody would go thirsty. **"What can we do about it?"** sighed Sydney.

Brainstorming, Sydney started drawing her ideas. After many tries, she sketched one that they both liked.

Zhi proposed, "But we'll need more muscle to do this." Together they convinced their neighbors to help.

In the coming days,
the gang journeyed into the
wilderness to share Sydney's plan with the other animals. Naturally, everyone wasn't used to cooperating. Yet, big and small, they agreed to lend a hand.

The next morning, they all met at the dam. Inspecting several loose logs nearby, they finally carried one back to the riverbed. Zhi poked at the wall with her staff.

"Stick it into this gap," she suggested.

With the wooden lever firmly in place, one by one they climbed aboard. Teetering on the beam, they leapt up and down. When they hopped at the same time, pebbles popped out and then some rocks.

Again and again they jumped. Yet they were getting tired, and a few of them were losing hope. "We can't give up now," Zhi urged.

"C'mon, one more time," pleaded Sydney. **"3, 2, 1...** ***Baaa Baaa!"***

--

Crack! Out bounded a boulder and a fountain spurted into the air.

Whoosh! A rush of water broke through the dam and the animals clambered onto the banks. The river flowed again!

The unlikely partners could enjoy their common achievement and a well-deserved rest.

The bunch received hearty congratulations from friends and family alike.

Downstream, the grasses gradually regained their green, and the meadow flowers bloomed. Mama and Papa realized their daughter was growing up in her own special way and were quite pleased.

Sydney and Zhi continued to roam far and wide... and sometimes find themselves in sticky situations.

Warm and generous with others, Sydney liked coming up with fresh approaches and always tried to do her part.

Sydney and Zhi were best
buddies who watched each other's
back, took unusual strolls, and always
swung for the fences. And everyone agreed it was a fantastic Year of the Sheep.

羊

Sheep
1919, 1931, 1943, 1955, 1967, 1979, 1991, 2003, 2015, 2027

People born in the Year of the Sheep are approachable, easy-going, and cooperative. They are kind-hearted, down-to-earth, and creative. But they can be shy, tend to go with the flow, and need a bit of guidance. Though they like the routine comforts of home, sheep are nurturing and giving pals.